A Very Mouse Tale

Robyn North

Text and Illustrations © 1994 Robyn North

Book layout by Hilde G. Lee, Hildesigns
Printed in Hong Kong

Library of Congress Cataloging in Publication Data
ISBN 0-9643731-0-6

Robin Books
Free Union, Virginia

In the wall boards of the Wiley's garage,
Mr. Mouse let out a little sigh.
"Oh dear," he said, "More bad weather
on the way."
He put down the newspaper he was
reading.
"We had better go out to get some more
food.
The cupboard next door in the Wiley's
kitchen is out of bounds.
Millicent, the cat, is always watching for
us with her never blinking, big yellow
eyes."

"No matter how quickly we dash across the kitchen floor she is sure to see us," said Mrs. Mouse.

She put the children's breakfast in acorn bowls.

"All we have is corn.

The little ones are sick of eating corn every day.

We must go out into the street to look for some food."

Mr. Mouse put a little bag on his shoulder.

"We will go to the baker's shop and fill the bag with crumbs."

"Uncle Barney, WAKE UP, you must look after the children," said Mrs. Mouse.

"Dear Uncle Barney, do mind the children while we are out.

See that they don't stray into the kitchen.

Did he mumble yes?

Oh dear he is asleep again.

He has eaten too much corn for breakfast.

That cat — beware of that cat, Millicent, children.

She is always looking for a meal and mice are her favorite dish."

"Well, fuzzle my fur, there she is looking in," said Mrs. Mouse.
"I think we will leave by the back door.
Children do not tease Millicent.
You are making me nervous.
Come father, we must leave by the back door through the garage.
The world is such a dangerous place for mice."

They scrambled out into the street and
blinked in the bright morning light.
"What a wild and wonderful day.
It is so good to feel the breeze in my fur,"
said Mrs. Mouse.
"But we must hurry. It is dangerous in
the street.
Mind that car, I think it is about to move.
We must be careful of the puddles. I
don't feel like a swim."

"Mercy me, there is another pussy cat," said Mr. Mouse.
"I think it has seen us.
Run, Mrs. Mouse, run.
Hurry, hurry we must hide."
Mr. Mouse took her hand, and they ran until their sides ached, not daring to look back.
"My soul," panted Mr. Mouse, "I can see a big dog coming. Do dogs like mice?"
"I would rather not think about it," gasped Mrs. Mouse.
"I know they don't like cats."

At last, almost completely out of
breath, they arrived at the bakery.
"What a long line.
We can't possibly wait to be served,"
remarked Mrs. Mouse.
"Just look at those delicious cakes.
They make my mouth water.
Wouldn't that large bird looking in the
window just love to pick the cherries
off that chocolate cake?"

They scurried into the pantry and soon
filled the bag with crumbs.
Mr. and Mrs. Mouse tossed a few sugary
crumbs in the air with glee.
"We will eat well tonight," Father Mouse
squealed.
Then they climbed onto the shelves of the
pantry.
"Where are you Mrs. Mouse?" he shouted.

"Help, help!," cried Mrs. Mouse.
"I've fallen into the bowl of whipped
cream.
All I wanted was a little taste, but oh dear,
I've fallen in.
The cream is delicious, but I must climb
out before I sink."
"Here is my tail. Grab hold of it and
hold tight," said Mr. Mouse. He
pulled with all his might until he
thought his poor tail would fall off.
At last Mrs. Mouse was able to scramble
out of the bowl.

She was licking her fur clean when she
heard Mr. Mouse squeal.
"My dear, come here at once," he
called as he popped his head out
of the little gingerbread house.
"Delight of my life, this is the kind of
home I have always longed to give
you."
"Ah yes," said Mrs. Mouse, admiring it.
"But I love the house so much I would
probably eat it."
She broke off a sugary flower from the
sweet garden and started to nibble it
as they went into the house.

Then Mr. and Mrs. Mouse heard
Melissa Wiley's loud voice in the shop.
"Why does she think we are all deaf?"
asked Mrs. Mouse, putting her fingers
in her ears.
"There it is Mom. I want that gingerbread
house for my birthday cake."
"It's a little bit expensive,dear," said her
mother.
"But I want it, I want it," Melissa moaned.
"We will take it," said Mrs. Wiley to the
baker, so he carefully put the ginger
bread house in a large box.
"Spoiled child," he muttered to himself,
but the mice heard it.

The mice had a dark and bumpy journey inside the gingerbread house. Presently there was a scraping sound of a door opening and then all was quiet.

"I think we are in the kitchen, because I can hear the faucet dripping," said Mr. Mouse.

"You are clever, my dear, but what can we do?" asked Mrs. Mouse

"We must settle down until the Wileys have gone to bed.

Now we must have a nap. The hole I chewed in the wall has filled me up. We need to rest before we chew our way out of this box," Mr. Mouse yawned.

Next morning Melissa Wiley came into the kitchen and peeped into the box at the gingerbread house.

"My beautiful cake," she screamed.

"Those disgusting mice have eaten it."

"Oh what a pity," exclaimed Mrs. Wiley, looking very cross.

"We will have to throw it out. I have a cream sponge cake in the freezer. That will have to do."

But Melissa continued crying.

"Tut, tut, those mice," Mrs. Wiley muttered, as she put the gingerbread house in the garage for the garbage collection.

Mr. Mouse put his head out of his
door to get a breath of fresh air and
saw the box.

"Well, dreams are made of this," he said
when he looked into the box and saw
the gingerbread house.

"Wake up children. I have a surprise for
you."

He tugged at the laces of Melissa's old
gym shoe.

"Get out of bed we are going to have a
party."

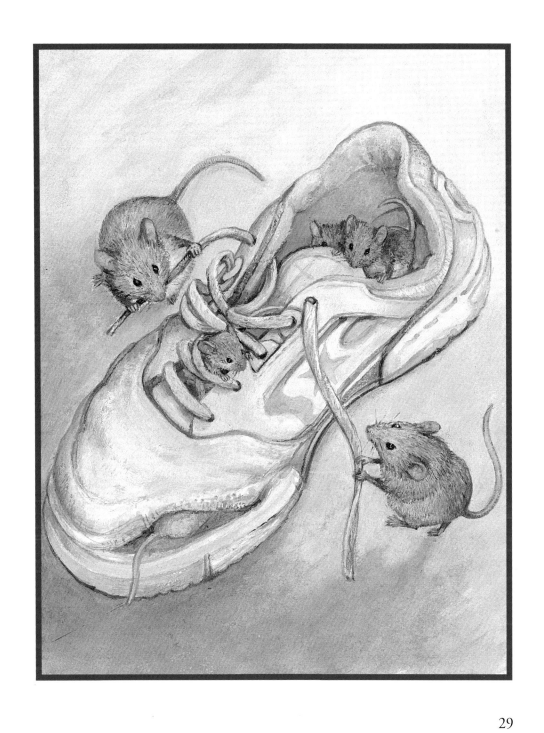

And what a mouse party it was.

There was just one thing troubling Mrs. Mouse.

"I don't think the Wileys are fond of us," she said.

"We must be very quiet for a while."

"That will be easy," sighed Uncle Barney, rubbing his plump tummy.

"We have lots of gingerbread to eat," he said as he began munching on the chimney."

The End